Dear Parents:

The **Ready Reader Storybooks**™ were created especially for children in kindergarten through second grade. This series is designed to increase children's reading skills and promote their interest in reading by themselves. The stories are enjoyable, with easy-to-follow plot structures and familiar settings. Colorful illustrations help develop young imaginations while adding visual appeal to the reading experience. Young children will be comfortable with the format and the large type.

With a variety of stories to accommodate individual interests, the **Ready Reader Storybooks**™ can help develop basic abilities and encourage your children's independent reading.

Walter
and the
Tugboat

Written by Eugene Bradley Coco
Illustrated by Edward Heck

Modern Publishing
A Division of Unisystems, Inc.
New York, New York 10022

This is Walter the whale.

Walter lives in the deep, blue sea.

Walter likes to do many things.

He likes to splash in the waves,
and spout water high in the sky.

He likes to play tag
with his friends.

But most of all,
Walter likes to watch tugboats
pull ships through the sea.

Big ships.

Little ships.

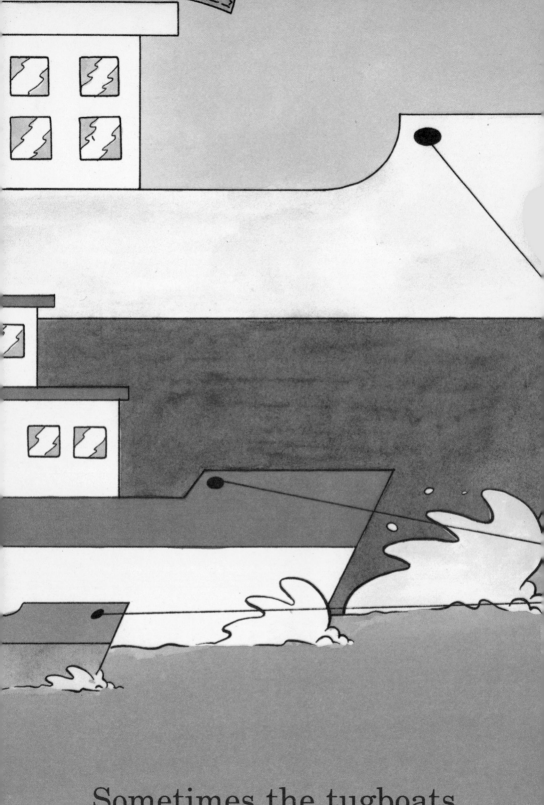

Sometimes the tugboats

even pull two or three ships.

Here comes a tugboat now.

Walter waves his tail
as it passes by.

Captain Jim waves back.

"I want to be a tugboat,"
says Walter.

"I want to pull ships along
the sea like you do."

"You can't be a tugboat,"
laughs Captain Jim,
"you're a whale."

One day Walter sees Captain Jim's tugboat far out at sea.

Something is wrong.

Captain Jim's
tugboat is not tugging.

Walter swims out to
the tugboat as fast as he can.

"My tugboat is not big enough to pull this ship," says Captain Jim.

Walter puts the rope in his mouth and, with all of his might,

pulls the ship to safety.

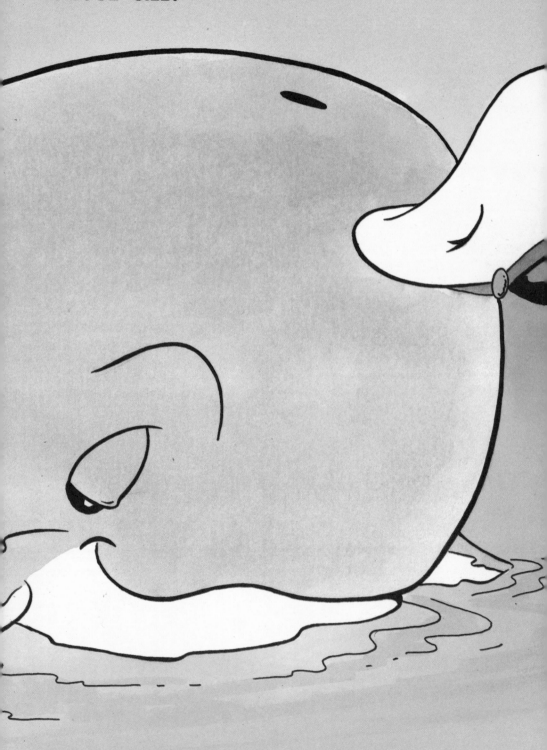

Walter smiles.
He is happy.

Now he is a tugboat too.